This book belongs to

....

....

'To Lilly with love' Frank Endersby

This edition first published in 2019 by Alligator Products Ltd.
Cupcake is an imprint of Alligator Products Ltd.
2nd Floor, 314 Regents Park Road, London N3 2JX

Written by Christine Swift
Illustrated by Frank Endersby

Printed in China.1539

Little Bear Won't Sleep!

cupcake

Little Bear did not want to go to sleep. He just wasn't tired.

"You must go to sleep," said his mother, "or you'll be too tired to play tomorrow."

Little Bear didn't care, "I want to stay up all night!" he said.

Mother Bear smiled softly. "Let's go for a walk!" she said.
"We can walk ALL night!" Little Bear thought this was a
fantastic idea ...

He could count the stars ...

he could look for a shooting star ...

or he could chase after the bats!

The moon was bright in the sky and there were noises all around – from the rustling of the leaves in the wind to the night-time animals moving about in the forest.

Little Bear jumped up excitedly, thinking of all the fun he could have and all the friends he could make.

Twit-twoo!

They didn't have to go far before they heard, "Twit-twoo."
It was an owl in the tree.
Owl spun his head round. "Hello," he said. "Isn't it your
bedtime, Little Bear?"

"Not tonight," smiled Little Bear, "I'm staying up ALL night!"

In the moonlight, Little Bear saw
something move.
Something very quick indeed came
bounding up to him.
"Good evening," said the fox.
"I can't stop, I'm busy looking for
breakfast!" and off he went.

Good evening!

Little Bear thought about breakfast. He was beginning to feel a little hungry!

They reached a clearing in the forest, "Let's rest here for a moment," said Mother Bear. They sat and looked at the stars glistening in the night sky. Flying above them, Little Bear saw lots of bats.

"I know you're there, Little Bear," Bat said. "You should be in bed. It's far too late for you to be wandering around the forest!"

"Not tonight," smiled Little Bear. "I'm staying up ALL night tonight!"

Ouch!

"No!" squeaked Little Bear, as he tried to hide a tiny,
tiny yawn! There was something rustling among the leaves and
Little Bear felt around with his paw to find out what it was.
"Ouch!" he cried.

"Be careful, Little Bear," said Mother Bear.
"That's a hedgehog and they can be very prickly indeed."
"That's right," said the hedgehog. "I'm looking for
something delicious to eat among these leaves.
Now if you can move your paw Little Bear,
I'll be on my way!"